The Mysterious Midnight Visitor

That night, Nan snuggled down under her blankets. Her windows were wide open, so she could smell the salt air on the breeze.

She started to drift off into a quiet . . . gentle . . .

What was that?

Nan sat up and looked across the bed at the window.

A figure draped in white was trying to break into her room!

Books in The New Bobbsey Twins series

Available from MINSTREL Books

THE NEW
Bobbsey Twins™
Twins™

#4
THE SECRET IN THE SAND CASTLE

LAURA LEE HOPE

ILLUSTRATED BY PAUL JENNIS

A
MINSTREL™
BOOK

PUBLISHED BY POCKET BOOKS

A MINSTREL PAPERBACK *ORIGINAL*

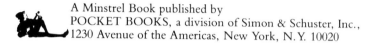 A Minstrel Book published by
POCKET BOOKS, a division of Simon & Schuster, Inc.,
1230 Avenue of the Americas, New York, N.Y. 10020

ISBN: 0-671-62654-X

Produced by Mega-Books of New York, Inc.

First Minstrel Books printing February, 1988

10 9 8 7 6 5 4 3 2 1

THE NEW BOBBSEY TWINS, A MINSTREL BOOK and colophon are trademarks of Simon & Schuster, Inc.

THE BOBBSEY TWINS is a registered trademark of Simon & Schuster, Inc.

Printed in the U.S.A.

Contents

THE SECRET
IN THE SAND
CASTLE

1

The Ghost in the Parlor

"Wow! Look at that! It's like gingerbread," said Flossie Bobbsey. She stared at the old white house with the green lawn sweeping down to the bay.

"All you ever think about is food," her twin brother, Freddie, said. "I can't wait to go to the beach. I bet I'll find a million shells down there."

Their father opened the back of the station wagon and sighed. "Between four bicycles and our clothes, it looks like we're staying for a year. Remember, we're only at Beachcliff Bay for a few weeks. Okay, kids, let's unload this stuff."

Twelve-year-old Bert Bobbsey picked up a carton marked "Art Supplies." He handed it to his twin sister, Nan.

"This is yours," he said. "You put it on top of my Rex Sleuther kit."

But Nan was too busy staring at the big white house to respond.

"The house is kind of weird looking, isn't it? All those fancy cutouts and frills. Why did they do all that?" she asked her father.

Mr. Bobbsey had come to Beachcliff Bay to help out a local home builder. His job was to find those antique wooden cutouts—or make new ones. Since he owned a lumberyard, wood was something he knew a great deal about.

"Years ago, people who owned these big houses all tried to outdo each other," Mr. Bobbsey said. "The more frills, the better."

The wind shifted and a breeze swept across the bay.

Nan laughed. "Some of the frills are rusty. The weather vane didn't budge."

"You're right," Freddie said. "That whale is still pointing to the beach."

"Well, you all just point yourselves in the direction of these boxes," said Mrs. Bobbsey. "Somewhere in Beachcliff Bay there's an unusual story, and I have to find it. Or else I'll have nothing to send back to the *Lakeport News*."

Mrs. Bobbsey was a part-time reporter for their hometown newspaper. She had promised to come up with a story for the Travel section.

"Let's get everything inside," she went on. "Then you kids can set up your own rooms. Who wants to go first?"

"Hah!" said Freddie. "Flossie's already upstairs, picking the biggest room."

While Bert and Nan were laughing, a car pulled up. "Here's Jim Reade now," Mr. Bobbsey said. Mr. Reade was the man who had hired Mr. Bobbsey to help him out.

"Well, looks like we finished fixing up this place just in time," said Mr. Reade as he got out of his car. "Wilson House is our first crack at renovation. Too bad we had to do it without your expert eye."

As Mr. Bobbsey reached forward to shake Mr. Reade's hand, a piercing shriek came from inside the house. Then Flossie darted out the front door.

"I saw it! I saw it! It was horrible," she cried.

"What? Darling, tell us what you saw," said Mrs. Bobbsey, hugging Flossie.

"I saw a ghost. No, really, I did!" Flossie insisted. "It was white and flapping and—"

"Oh, no," said Mr. Reade, smiling. "Every old house in this town has a ghost. And Wilson House *is* the most famous. Still, I've never heard of ghosts running around in broad daylight."

"There's the answer," Bert said, pointing at the front door.

An old man in overalls struggled down the front walk. He carried an armload of white sheets that billowed in the breeze.

"See here, now," the stranger said. "Who was doing that screaming? Never heard such a confounded noise. There I was, trying to get these sheets off the furniture and the place all aired out. Next thing I knew, I heard such a yelling, I almost dropped my teeth."

"Flossie!" said Freddie. "Can't you tell the difference between a ghost and a sheet?"

"Well," Flossie said, "how come it was walking toward me and waving its arms?"

"I'll tell you one thing," Mr. Reade said. "I'm relieved. I was afraid I'd see a smaller shape under those sheets."

"A smaller ghost?" whispered Flossie.

"My son, Jimmy," Mr. Reade said. "He was supposed to come up and give Pete a hand. But I guess a ten-year-old boy has better things to do on a sunny day like today."

"Last I looked, he was headed down toward the beach," the man carrying the sheets said. "Wearing that Micro-Man T-shirt of his."

"Micro-Man? *The* Micro-Man, the Human Computer?" said Freddie.

"If you like Micro-Man, you'll get along fine with Jimmy," Mr. Reade said. "He's going to make a giant Micro-Man space fortress for our local sand-castle building contest. Says it'll win first prize."

"Let's enter the contest, too!" Freddie shouted.

"Maybe we will," Bert said. "But, Mr. Reade, why did you think Jimmy might be the ghost?"

"He loves listening to Pete's stories. By the way, let me introduce Pete Smedley. Pete works for Reade Realty. He's looked after Wilson House since it was abandoned. That was about the time the so-called ghosts moved in."

"Yep," Pete said. "That was when the last Wilson left this place. Guess the old house just don't want anyone else living in it."

"Why did the Wilsons leave?" asked Bert.

"Don't suppose they wanted to. But there was some trouble. They drowned out there in the bay. Ever since, the ghosts of Clay and Jennie Wilson keep prowling through the house. 'Specially when the moon is full and there's a breeze coming in from the bay."

"Really?" Flossie asked. "How do you know that?"

"'Cause they move things around. And sometimes they leave a trail. You know, seaweed and shells and salt water, all over," Pete said, shaking his head. "Makes all sorts of work for me to come and clean up afterward."

"Look," Mr. Reade said, "you can't expect an old house to be airtight. And if a window's left open, or a draft blows down the chimney— well, a lot of things just happen."

"Right!" Mrs. Bobbsey said. "But those soggy old Wilsons are going to have to make room for the Bobbseys. We're not going to let a few flapping sheets ruin our vacation."

"I'm sure the house is ready," Mr. Reade said. "And you won't be bothered by ghosts."

"Might as well take these sheets over to the laundry," Pete said. He headed for the rusty brown pickup truck parked across the street.

"Say, would you all mind finishing up the moving-in?" Mr. Bobbsey said. "You could ex-

7

plore the house while I go down to Jim's office."

"Why don't you go, too, Mom?" Nan said. "We'll unload the car and set things up in our rooms. You could start snooping around for your story."

"I don't snoop," Mrs. Bobbsey said. "I investigate. But it would be nice to get started. If you really think you could take care of—"

"We can handle it," said Bert.

"Don't forget to unpack the cooler and put away the milk," called Mrs. Bobbsey as she got into Mr. Reade's car.

"Might as well get started," said Nan.

For the next half hour, the two sets of twins worked hard. They emptied the station wagon. Then they separated their belongings into four piles.

"I'm going to take my things to my room," Flossie said. "You'll be right next to it, Nan. We can share the big bathroom."

"Right," Nan said, chuckling to herself. "And I bet I know who has the best view of the beach."

"Well, you can see some of the water on your side," Flossie said. "If you sort of look around the corner."

"Come on, Freddie," Bert said. "We'd better

grab some space for ourselves. Or else, we'll end up in broom closets."

Later, in his room, Bert looked up and saw Flossie trying to drag something down the hall. It was a large mirror in a fancy, gilded frame.

"Hey, where are you going with that?" he called out.

"Nan and I need this," she said. "It was in the corner at the end of the hall. I guess they put it there to hide the pink flowers on the wallpaper that don't match the rest."

"Here, let me give you a hand."

"Thanks," said Flossie, puffing a bit from her efforts.

"Look, there's no way to hang it now," Bert said. He took the mirror from Flossie and carried it into her room. "Let's leave it here until we can find a hammer and nails." Carefully, he set the mirror down on the bed.

Nan and Freddie finished unpacking. Then they came into Flossie's room.

"You've got the biggest room here," said Freddie.

"I guess so," said Flossie, smiling.

"Oh, no!" Nan said. "We forgot to unpack the cooler. We'd better do that right now."

"And have chocolate milk," Freddie said. "I saw you pack the syrup, Floss."

9

"Race you down," said Flossie.

They all dashed downstairs to the big kitchen. Flossie reached the cooler first. She brought the milk and syrup over to the table.

"Wait!" said Bert. He wiped a thick layer of dust off the table with a sponge.

"Doesn't look like ghosts ate at this table lately," said Freddie.

A loud crash startled them.

"Wh-what was that?" said Flossie.

"Come on," Bert said. "We'll all go up together."

Bert charged up the stairs, but Flossie trailed behind. The house was very quiet. They went into Nan's room first. Everything was just as she had left it.

They went into the bathroom and opened the door to Flossie's room.

They all saw it at once. There, in the middle of Flossie's bed was the mirror, just where Bert had put it.

But now it was broken. Hundreds of little pieces gleamed in the sunlight that streamed through the window.

2

A Disappearing Book

"What a mess!" said Freddie, staring at the broken mirror.

"What happened?" Flossie moaned. "Do you think the ghosts did it?"

"Ghosts again!" groaned Nan. "Bert, did you notice anything strange when you put the mirror down?"

"No," Bert said. "And I was really careful." He thought for a second. "Maybe it had a lot of hairline cracks. And when we moved it, a chain reaction started. I mean, it has to be a really old mirror."

"I'll take that over 'ghosts' anytime," said Nan. "But we can't leave it on Flossie's bed."

"Oh, well, I brought the mirror in, I might as well lug the mess out," Bert said. "Give me a hand, Nan. If we pick it up by the frame we can carry it downstairs and out the back."

"Strange old house, isn't it?" said Nan. She and Bert inched down the stairs.

"All that molding and carving inside, too," Bert said. "I wonder what the first Wilsons were like, to build a place like this."

"Open the back door, Freddie," said Nan. Freddie pulled open the door, and Nan and Bert went out onto the back porch. They set the mirror down on a table.

"It should be okay here, for a while," Bert said. "I'll find Pete and ask him what to do next."

"I'm getting interested in Wilson House," Nan said. "Anyone want to ride over to the library with me?"

"I will," Freddie said. "But what for?"

"Because I'll bet they have some information on this place. Anyone else want to come?"

"Not me," Bert said. "I'm going to read Rex Sleuther to see if he says anything about mirrors." Rex Sleuther was a detective and the hero of his own comic book. Bert was his biggest fan.

Flossie shook her head. "I want to finish fixing my room."

Nan and Freddie rode into town and found the Beachcliff Bay Library on Main Street. It was right across from the fish market and the hardware store. They parked their bikes and went inside.

The first thing they saw was a sign—BEACH-CLIFF BAY HISTORY—with a black arrow pointing to a flight of narrow stairs.

"Nan, look!" Freddie said, and raced up the stairs. Nan followed him.

They were soon seated at a round oak table, with piles of books about Beachcliff Bay in front of them.

"Here," Nan said, holding a large book with a pea-soup green cover. "Look, it has a whole chapter on the Wilsons. They were one of the first families to settle here."

"Does it say anything about the house?" Freddie asked. "Wait, isn't that a picture?"

"Mmmmm," Nan said. "One of the earliest. Before they added on to it. That big willow tree isn't there anymore. Wait a sec, here's another picture, a later one. That looks a lot more like it."

"Does it say anything about ghosts?"

"No, but here's something on the last of the Wilson family. Oh, wow! That's awful."

"What's the matter?" asked Freddie.

"There's a lot more than Pete told us. The last Wilsons were a brother and sister, Clay and Jennie. They were artists. She painted and he was a sculptor."

"A what?"

"He made statues," Nan said. "In fact, he made that giant thing out in front of the library."

"That?" Freddie said. "I thought it was a stack of old coat hangers and junk for a scrap drive. Like we have for the Cub Scouts."

"Seems like Clay and Jennie had a big problem," Nan continued. "They spent more money than they earned. It costs a lot to make one of those huge sculptures, I guess. Anyhow, the Wilsons were broke. So Clay and Jennie did something awful. They stole a shipment of gold bars from an armored car!"

"You're kidding," Freddie said. "Did they get away with it?"

"No, and here comes the really bad part. It took awhile, but the police went after them. Clay and Jennie tried to get away by boat, but it capsized. It was during one of the worst storms in the history of Beachcliff Bay."

"They drowned?"

"Must have. The bodies were never found. Neither was the boat. Nor the gold."

"Wow!" Freddie whispered. "Sunken treasure!"

"Not really," Nan said. "According to this book, the police believed Clay and Jennie hid the gold before they took off in the storm."

"Maybe that's why they came back as ghosts. To keep an eye on their gold," said Freddie.

"Hmm," Nan said. "This is a great picture of the house. I have an idea. Remember that sand-castle contest Mr. Reade was talking about? What if we made a sand-castle copy of Wilson House?"

"It would sure take a lot of work," said Freddie.

"But we could practice out on the beach. It would be fun. Why don't we try to get a better picture to work from? You know, we probably should have looked under *W* in the card catalog. There might be a book just on the Wilsons or Wilson House."

Freddie shrugged. "I'll just look on the shelves," he said.

Nan headed for the stack of oak file boxes and started looking through the *W* cards.

"There's nothing under *Wilson*," she said.

"What's that noise?" Freddie said. He looked

out the window. "Someone's just knocked over our bikes. The wheels are still spinning."

He ran downstairs. Nan jumped up and looked out the window. Someone ran around the corner toward the back of the library. Freddie dashed after him.

"What's going on?" asked a voice. Nan turned. A woman stood in the doorway of the small room.

"I'm Mrs. Morris, the librarian," the woman said. "Is that boy who just ran out with you? And what are you doing with all these books?"

Nan started to explain when a loud noise exploded from downstairs.

"That can only be books falling over," Mrs. Morris said. "I'd know that sound anywhere!"

She and Nan rushed down the narrow stairs. At the rear of the library Freddie and a red-headed boy were shouting at each other. A cartful of books lay scattered on the floor between them.

"It's your fault!" the boy shouted. "You ran into the cart."

"You started it!" Freddie yelled. "You knocked over our bikes."

"I don't care who started what," said the librarian. "I want this mess cleaned up right now." A door behind the two boys opened.

"Mr. Reade!" said Nan.

"Dad," said the boy.

"Jimmy?" said Freddie, looking at the boy.

"I come for you and find this?" Mr. Reade said. "A fine way to meet the Bobbseys. I told you about them this morning."

"Big deal," muttered Jimmy.

"I'll wait in the car. We'll talk when you're through picking up those books." Mr. Reade went out.

The damage wasn't as bad as it looked. Jimmy set the book cart upright. Nan and Freddie began to pick up the books. But before they were all off the floor, Jimmy said, "Gotta check out something." He wandered off.

At last they were finished.

"I've had enough of the library to last me a long time," said Freddie.

"Me, too," Nan said. She placed the last book on the cart. "Let's get the book with the picture of Wilson House and leave."

They headed for the small room upstairs where they had left the books on Beachcliff Bay. When they got there, Freddie dashed for the oak table and stopped.

The book with the pea-soup green cover was gone.

18

3

Digging for Gold

"It was right there on top of the table!" said Freddie.

"Looks like all the others are still here," Nan said. She flipped through them quickly. "But none of them has a picture of the Wilson house. I'm going to ask Mrs. Morris if someone checked the book out while we were putting those other books back on the cart." She returned in a few minutes with Mrs. Morris.

"I'm sure no one checked it out," Mrs. Morris said. "The Beachcliff Bay section isn't that big. Let's have a thorough look to make sure."

They combed the shelves in the little room. They looked under tables and chairs.

The book was definitely missing.

"It looks as if someone came in while my back was turned and took the book," said Mrs. Morris.

Nan and Freddie looked at each other. The same thought came to both minds: Jimmy.

"My husband is the deputy police chief. I'm going to tell him about this," she continued. She went back to her desk.

Nan and Freddie went outside and got on their bikes.

"Is your bicycle okay?" Nan asked.

Freddie checked his bike carefully. "I think one spoke is bent a little," he said. "But it's all right."

"Let's stop by Mr. Reade's office," Nan said. "Maybe the little sneak is over there."

"Yeah," Freddie said. "With *our* book. Wonder why he didn't just check it out. Why did he have to steal it?"

"Let's find out."

But the visit to Reade Realty didn't give them any answers.

"I took Jimmy straight home. And he didn't have a book with him," Mr. Reade said. "I would have noticed if he did. Jimmy doesn't like to read books."

"Then why did he go to the library?" asked Freddie.

Mr. Reade sighed. "So he wouldn't have to do his chores. He was hiding there. And that only got him in trouble. Now, if you don't mind, I've got work to do."

Nan and Freddie left Mr. Reade and headed for the house.

"I don't like Mr. Reade," said Freddie.

"Neither do I," Nan said. "But I don't think he was lying. Jimmy didn't take the book."

When Nan and Freddie got back to the house, Bert said, "We've come up with a great idea."

"We want to have a clambake," said Flossie.

"It would make a great surprise for Mom and Dad," Bert said. "We can dig a pit on the beach and collect driftwood for a fire. Then we can bike into town to buy the corn and the clams and all that stuff."

"I've made a list," said Flossie.

"Here, let me see," Nan said. "I hate shopping, but it's better than digging ditches. Come with me, Flossie. We'll get the food now."

After they left, Bert and Freddie went to work. They dug a deep pit in the sand. Then they covered the bottom with rocks.

"Now we have to gather seaweed," said Bert.

"What for?" asked Freddie.

"To line the pit." Bert looked around. "Maybe there's some over here. . . ."

"Thought you'd need some buckets." The voice came from a nearby sand dune.

"Buckets?" asked Bert. Pete Smedley was standing on top of the dune.

"To haul back the gold. Diggin' for gold, ain't you? That's what I figure you're up to."

"What?" said Bert.

"Yep, keep on lookin' for that Wilson gold," muttered Pete as he wandered back toward the big white house.

"Wilson gold?" said Bert.

"Yeah," said Freddie. He told Bert what he and Nan had found out in the library. And everything that had happened afterward.

Bert laughed. "It's a great story, but we've got a clambake to set up. We can worry about the missing book and the gold afterward."

Later, at the house, Bert said, "That old guy sure is hung up on that gold, isn't he?"

"Kind of silly, isn't it?"

"Still, you never know. . . ." said Bert.

"Might be worth giving it a try," said Freddie.

"Just for fun," said Bert.

"'Course," said Freddie.

"But I'd feel dumb digging up flower beds."

"Or the lawn."

"Hey," Bert said. "What about that old root cellar? You know, the one we found when we were looking for the shovels?"

"Right," Freddie said. "It leads into the back of the house. Only it doesn't go anywhere."

"And it has a dirt floor," Bert said. "Come on."

The two boys opened the hatch doors and climbed down into the root cellar. They had just begun to dig into the rich, brown earth when the hatch doors slammed down. They were in total darkness.

Carefully, Freddie made his way to the doors.

"Bert," he said, "I can't open them!"

"Let me try." Bert pushed up on them, too.

"Push hard!" said Freddie.

"I am," Bert said. "Something's stuck through the handles. Wait a minute, I've got my Rex Sleuther knife."

"What can you do with that?"

"I'll use the saw blade to cut our way out."

24

"Great!" said Freddie.

"Not so great." Bert sighed. "It's not even making a dent. That bar is metal."

"You mean . . ." whispered Freddie.

"Yes," his brother answered. "We're trapped."

4

The Mysterious Visitor

"It's a good thing we both went shopping," Flossie said. "You'd never be able to carry all this stuff alone."

The bag of groceries on Flossie's bicycle was almost as big as the one on Nan's. Nan laughed.

"I might not have had so much to carry if I'd gone alone," Nan said. "Since when is taffy part of a clambake?"

"It's saltwater taffy," said Flossie.

"Okay, okay." Nan sighed.

They walked their bikes up to the front of the Wilson house.

"These bags are all yucky from the clams," said Flossie.

"Maybe we'd better go in the back way," said Nan.

Carrying their bags of food, the two girls headed for the back of the house. Halfway there Nan stopped.

"What's that banging noise?" she asked.

Flossie looked around. "I don't know," she said.

"Maybe Pete what's-his-name is doing some work," Nan said, walking on.

"Or maybe," Flossie said, "it's the . . . you know . . ."

"What?"

"Ghosts!" Flossie whispered.

The banging got louder. And as the girls reached the backyard, they heard shouts.

"Too noisy for ghosts," Nan said. "It seems to be coming from over there."

"From the root cellar?" asked Flossie.

"Looks like it," Nan said, putting down her bag. "And it sounds like Bert and Freddie!"

Nan rushed over to the root cellar. She pulled out the pipe stuck through the door handles.

"Whoops!" cried Nan. The doors flew open. Bert and Freddie charged up the stairs.

"What are you guys doing down there?" asked Flossie.

"Never mind that," Bert said. "I'd like to know who locked us in."

He examined the pipe.

"Oh, rats, your fingerprints are all over it. It's smudged," he said.

"What's going on?" asked Nan.

Before Bert could open his mouth, Freddie blurted out the whole story.

"And you didn't find the buried gold." Flossie sighed.

"Forget the digging. We have to get this stuff inside or we'll never be ready for the clambake," said Nan.

"But what about finding out who locked us in?" asked Freddie.

"I'm sure whoever did it isn't hanging around," said Nan.

They picked up the groceries and walked into the house.

"Guys," Nan said. "I left that cooler open so it would dry. Why'd you close it and stick it in the corner?"

"I didn't touch it," said Bert.

"Neither did I," said Freddie.

"Well, who put these cookies in the refrigerator?" asked Flossie. She was putting the groceries away.

"Where are all the canned things? I left them out so Mom could decide where to put them," said Nan.

"Here they are, under the sink," said Bert, poking around.

"Did you guys put them in there?" asked Nan.

"Uh-uh," said the boys.

"Not me," said Flossie.

They stared at each other.

"Know what I think?" said Nan. "Someone's been in here."

"Someone locked us in to get us out of the way," Freddie said. "So the coast would be clear . . ."

"To search the premises!" said Bert.

"And that," Nan said, "is just what we should do. Let's see if any of our stuff has been messed with."

They raced upstairs, Flossie and Bert in the lead. At the landing, Flossie paused.

"Do you hear something funny?" she asked. "Listen."

Nan heard rustling and a faint bumping at the end of the hall. She and Flossie tiptoed in that direction. The boys went to check out the other rooms.

"The noises are getting fainter," Nan said.

There was a sudden loud thud. Both girls jumped.

"I think it's in the wall," Flossie said bravely. *Thud!*

"Hey, are you guys fooling around?" shouted Nan.

Bert and Freddie poked their heads out of Bert's room.

"I was just going to ask you that," said Bert.

"Do you think it could be . . . you know, the G-H-O-S-T?" Flossie whispered to Nan. "Or, maybe . . . ugh . . . R-A-T-S?"

Nan shook her head. "I'm going to check out my room. If anyone messed with my stuff, they're in big trouble."

She marched off down the hall.

Flossie looked around. Her eye fell on the wallpaper that didn't match.

"If you ghosts are in there," she said, "please stop trying to scare me." That reminded her of the broken mirror. She had found it right where she was standing. Just then something else caught her eye. It was a tiny rubber ring. She bent down and scooped it up.

She ran into Nan's room. "Look at this. I found it where the mirror used to be."

"Don't get so excited, Floss," Nan said. "It's just an old washer. One of the plumbers must have left it behind."

"But it wasn't there before," said Flossie.

"Flossie, try to relax. We're getting jumpy over nothing. As a matter of fact, I have an idea who locked the boys in and moved things around downstairs. It was that nasty Jimmy Reade, the one who knocked over our bikes."

"You really don't think it was a . . . you know?" said Flossie.

Nan grinned and hugged Flossie. "Let's get cleaned up. Then we'll take the stuff down to the beach. When Mom and Dad get back, we'll be all ready."

"I could use a bath. With some of that bubbly stuff you gave me for my birthday," said Flossie. She rushed into the bathroom.

"I know what I'm going to do," Nan said to herself. "I'm going to use that outdoor shower behind the barn. I'll have it all to myself while everyone's up here."

She put on her white terry-cloth robe. Then she found some clean clothes to change into. She took the biggest bath towel she could find and headed downstairs.

The outdoor shower was great. Lots of hot water. She washed her hair and was just rinsing it when she heard a loud, piercing scream. It came from inside the house. Through the steam and the spray, she could hear Flossie shrieking.

"EEEEEEEK! Someone, HELP ME!"

5

Door into Darkness

Nan pulled on her robe and threw the towel over her head. She raced toward the back door.

"It's the *ghost!*" Freddie shouted, running out of the house.

"Don't be silly," Nan said, pulling back the towel from her head. "What are you doing down here? Didn't you hear Flossie scream?"

"I was looking for her," said Freddie. "Isn't she with you?"

"She's upstairs," Nan said. "Taking a bath."

"No, she's not," said Freddie. "Bert and I already looked in your rooms."

"We'd better look downstairs, right now," said Nan.

They went inside and started poking around the kitchen. They opened every door and cupboard.

"Nothing," said Freddie.

"You try the dining room. I'll try the side of the house," said Nan. She covered her wet head with the towel.

Nan looked on the sun porch on the side of the house. Nothing there. Maybe behind that folding screen?

She started to back out of the doorway when she felt an arm around her throat and another around her waist.

"Aha, ghostie, I have you now!" cried the voice behind her.

"Bert," Nan shouted. "Let me go!"

"Oh, it's just you. . . ."

"Did you really think I was a ghost?" Nan asked.

Bert shrugged. "I hoped you were Flossie dressed up in Mom's shoes and robe."

"What was that?" asked Nan. "That bumping sound."

She dashed into the dining room. Bert and Freddie were close behind her.

Nan tiptoed around a corner. A figure in white was coming toward her. Nan jumped and let out a yell.

"What's the matter?" Freddie asked.

"Oh, Freddie," Nan said. She laughed nervously. "I saw myself in that mirror on the closet door. This house is crazy."

"I'll say," Bert said. "I went into the laundry room and found a door I thought was a closet. It led right into the living room, next to the fireplace. Weird!"

"Did you search the living room?" Nan asked.

Bert shook his head. "It was empty."

"Flossie's got to be in this house!"

"Come on," Bert said. "We'll all go through the living room together. It's sure big enough."

Nan checked the closet. Bert checked under the sofa, just in case Flossie was hiding. Freddie looked up the gigantic fireplace.

"Can I help?" asked Flossie. She was standing in the doorway.

Freddie whirled and tripped over the rug.

"Where have you been?" asked Bert.

"What happened?" said Nan.

"Look what you made me do!" said Freddie, rubbing a sore knee.

"You know I was going to take a bath? But I decided it would take too long. So I washed at the sink. And I changed into this sundress."

"Come on, Flossie, why did you scream?" Nan asked.

"You were still outside in the shower. And the boys were in their rooms. So I went exploring.

"Remember where I got the mirror and I found the rubber thing? And you know how I told you the wallpaper didn't match right? I went there and started looking around. And when I leaned on the wall where the mirror was, it moved. In."

"A hidden door!" said Nan.

"Wow," Bert said. "This is great!"

"What was behind the door?" asked Freddie.

"When I went inside, the door shut behind me. And that's when I yelled a little."

"'Yelled a little'?" Freddie said. "You screamed your head off!"

"Well, it was scary," Flossie said. "But I kept creeping along. And I had to go down a lot of stairs, too. It took forever, but I finally got to something that moved."

"Was it alive?" said Freddie.

"Silly," Flossie said. "It was a door. At the other end."

"Where'd you come out?" asked Bert.

"Come on," Flossie said. "I'll show you."

She led them out to the side of the house. Behind an overgrown tangle of bushes was a door. It had no handle.

"I'm going to get my flashlight and try it from up top," Bert said. "Come on, Flossie. Show me where you got in."

"I'm coming with you," said Nan.

"Me, too," shouted Freddie, running after them.

For the next half hour they explored the secret passage. It was an old stairway, dark and dusty.

"This must have been the back staircase," Nan said. "Nothing mysterious about that."

"Unless you were the only one who knew about it," Bert said. "This staircase may have always been a secret."

Flossie sneezed. "I'm getting hungry," she said.

"O my gosh," Nan said, "I still have to get dressed. And we've got a clambake to set up."

"You go ahead," Freddie said. "I'll meet you on the beach."

"Let's get going," said Bert. He went into the kitchen and picked up two bags of groceries.

Nan hurried into her clothes. Then she and Flossie picked up the rest of the food and walked to the beach.

"Hey, someone's at the pit," said Bert.

"It's Freddie!" said Flossie.

"How did you get here?" asked Nan.

"I found a secret passage, too," Freddie said, grinning. "See that tall grass over there? When I was here before with Bert, I noticed it was bent over. By the wind, I guess. It's like a small tunnel. I thought it might go all the way to the house. And it does."

"If we keep exploring secret passages we'll never get this clambake off the ground," Bert said. "Let's get to work."

"We could have found our way here just by the wonderful smells," said Mr. Bobbsey later on. He was on his second helping of clams steamed in seaweed.

"Everything is perfect," Mrs. Bobbsey said. "You kids are great cooks."

"You wouldn't believe all we did today," said Flossie.

"Probably not," said Mrs. Bobbsey.

Starting with the broken mirror, the twins recounted the day's events.

"Mr. Reade," Nan said, "wasn't very friendly."

"Things aren't going too well for him," said Mr. Bobbsey. "The houses he bought cost a lot of money to fix. Maybe that's made him a little jumpy. When we talked about Wilson House, he showed me the plans. I saw that secret passage you found, Flossie. It was the old servants' entrance. They must have papered over that area of the upstairs doorway."

"Did you meet Jimmy?" asked Freddie.

"No, why?" asked Mr. Bobbsey.

"I think he's a little sneak. I bet he tried to lock us in that root cellar."

"That's a nasty thing to do," Mr. Bobbsey said. "Are you sure he did it? Do you have any proof?" Bert and Freddie shook their heads.

"Do you think it was a . . . a ghost?" asked Flossie.

"Now, sweetie," said Mrs. Bobbsey. "Let's not get started on that again. Let's just enjoy the twilight."

"That's when *they* come out," whispered Freddie.

"Freddie!" snapped Nan. "There's no such thing as ghosts!"

When the last ray of daylight had disappeared, they put out the fire in the clambake pit. The Bobbseys gathered up their things and made their way home.

That night, Nan snuggled down under her blankets. Her windows were wide open, so she could smell the salt air on the breeze.

She burrowed deeper. The day's events flashed through her mind. The library. Pete and the flapping sheets. The root cellar. The broken mirror on Flossie's bed.

She started to drift off into a quiet, gentle . . . *What was that?*

She sat up and looked across the bed at the window.

A figure draped in white was trying to break into her room!

6

Ghosts?

As Nan's scream echoed down the hall, Mr. and Mrs. Bobbsey raced to her room. Flossie was right after them.

Mrs. Bobbsey leaned over Nan. She was huddled under the covers.

"Nan," she said gently. "What's wrong? Tell me what happened."

A hand crept out from under the blanket. A finger pointed toward the window.

"There's nothing there," said Mr. Bobbsey.

"Nothing?" said Nan. She sat up in bed.

"You must have been having a bad dream," said Mrs. Bobbsey.

"I wasn't asleep," Nan said. "Something was trying to get in."

They all went over to the window. Mr. Bobbsey examined the screen.

"The locks are still in place. I don't see any signs of an attempted break-in."

"But you can only see the inside, Dad," said Nan. She opened the screen. A piece of seaweed lay in a pool of water on the sill.

But there was nothing else to see. Through the darkness of the trees, the full moon shone brightly, casting long, long shadows.

At breakfast the next morning, everyone wanted to know about Nan's ghostly visitor.

Finally, Mr. Bobbsey said, "Enough of this ghost talk. As far as I'm concerned, there's only one important question. And that is, who put that pipe through the root cellar doors. Until we find out, I don't want any of you taking chances or being careless."

"You make it sound like it was our fault," said Bert.

"That's not what I mean," Mr. Bobbsey said.

"But digging for buried treasure is a little foolish, don't you think?"

Neither Bert nor Freddie said anything.

"Well, I'm off to see a man about some boards. Anyone care to come into town with me?" asked Mr. Bobbsey.

"I will," Mrs. Bobbsey said. "I'm still on the trail of a story. Beachcliff Bay is a pretty quiet place."

After they left, Bert turned to Nan and asked, "Did you really find seaweed on the sill?"

"It was the ghost, I just know it," Flossie said. "It came up out of the bay where it drowned."

"Maybe it *was* the Wilsons and they're mad because we're living in their house," said Freddie.

"And looking for their gold," added Flossie. "Only I'm not. And neither is Nan."

"Listen," Nan said. "The Wilsons aren't the only ones who don't want us here. I mean, we haven't exactly been welcomed."

"What do you mean?" asked Bert.

"First of all," Nan said, "there's Mr. Reade. Dad said he isn't in great shape financially. Maybe he's trying to scare us off so he can look for the gold."

47

"He acted as though he didn't like us when we were in his office," added Freddie.

"Or maybe he's just protecting his son, Jimmy," said Nan.

"But why would he be after the gold?" asked Freddie.

"Maybe because he's heard Pete's stories so many times," said Bert.

"Maybe it was Pete," said Flossie. "Remember how he scared me with the sheets?"

"That was an accident," Bert said. "He's got enough to keep him busy without bothering with us."

"I keep going back to Jimmy. Maybe it's not the gold. Maybe it's us," said Nan.

"But why?" asked Flossie.

"Okay, try this," Nan said. "Mr. Reade heard Bert say we might enter the sand-castle contest. He might have told Jimmy after he left here. So Jimmy decides that there are four of us to one of him. Bad odds. He'll scare us off. He knocks over our bikes. He steals our book. He locks Bert and Freddie in the root cellar. He—"

"He tries to break into your room?" asked Bert.

"Well," Nan said. "All of the pieces don't add up *exactly*. But I'll bet he's involved somehow."

"I'm sure of it," said Freddie.

"I'll tell you one thing," Nan said. "He's not

going to scare me away from that sand-castle contest. What do you say we all get to work on it now?"

"Uh, I have to do a few things in the shed first," said Bert.

"Flossie, come on," Freddie said. "There's something I want to show you."

"Okay," Nan said. "I'll just work on it by myself."

She dug into her art supplies and found her sketchbook. Then she went outside. With the bright morning sunlight striking the front of the house, Nan could see every detail. This sketch would be the perfect model for the sand castle, she thought. Nan noticed that the old weather vane was still pointing the same way.

She started to draw. A shadow stretched across her drawing, and she looked up. Suddenly the sky was filled with dark clouds. The sound of a ship's horn moaned from across the bay.

Nan felt a strange chill. It felt as if someone was standing right behind her. But she would have heard someone that close. Wouldn't she?

She turned her head slowly. She saw a bright flash. Someone *was* standing on the cliff just behind the house. Now he was gone. He had disappeared!

Nan shook her head. She blinked her eyes

several times. "I'm starting to see things."

She went back to work. She sketched in the roof. Then the trellis, which was broken . . .

Wait a minute! That trellis wasn't broken before. It was all right yesterday.

Nan put down her sketch pad and walked over to the house.

The trellis went right up to her bedroom window. It was like a ladder covered with roses. But now the roses hung loose as if they had been pulled off. And the slats in the trellis looked as if they'd snapped where someone had stepped on them.

Freddie and Flossie can talk about ghosts all they want, Nan thought. It was no ghost who broke that trellis. It was a person.

And a real-life person can be a lot more dangerous than a make-believe ghost.

7

"X Marks the Spot"

"Hey, Nan!" Bert shouted. He raced across the lawn.

She was staring up at the trellis.

"Look what I just found in the shed," he said. He carefully spread a map out in front of her. "It was tucked into a crack. See? It's an old map of Beachcliff Bay."

He pointed at various places on the map. "There's the beach, and the sand dunes, and the library, and the shopping area."

"What's this?" Nan's finger went to the top of the map. It showed a point of land that stretched out into the ocean. There was a big, black X across it.

"The name is faded," Bert said. "I can't read the first word. I think it's called something Neck."

Freddie and Flossie rode up on their bikes.

"Where have you kids been?" said Bert.

"At the library," Flossie said. "And wait till you hear the news."

"Right," Freddie said. "The bad news first. We went to the library to find that book with the picture. But it's still lost."

"Now the good news," Flossie added. "Mrs. Morris told us all about Wilson House. How Clay and Jennie stole the gold and everything."

"We know about that," Nan said.

"But she told us more. She said they weren't very nice," Flossie said. "Even if Clay did give that funny statue to the library."

"And he used to do his sculptures way off on the other side of town. He owned a shack on a piece of land with a funny name," said Freddie.

"It made me think of doughnuts," Flossie said. "Dunking Neck."

"That's it!" cried Bert. "Look!"

He pointed to the map. The piece of land sticking out into the water did look like a doughnut with a handle. He could just make out the faint letters D-N-K-N-G on the north side and, clearly, below, NECK.

"And right in the middle is 'X marks the spot.'" Freddie said. "That's where the gold must be hidden!"

"Can't argue with that," said Nan.

"I don't know about anyone else, but I'm going to take a ride out to Dunking Neck," said Bert.

"And I'm going with you," said Nan.

"We're coming, too," said Flossie.

They rushed off to get supplies and met back at their bikes. Bert carried the garden shovel. Nan had the map in her hands. Freddie had a trowel. Flossie had a napkin wrapped around some cookies.

"For later." She smiled.

They got on their bikes and pedaled about a mile.

Then Bert said, "There's a long stretch ahead. That must be Dunking Neck."

They were facing a strip of land with water on both sides.

"It's all sand here," Flossie said. "We won't be able to ride out to the end."

"It's not that far. I can see the shack down there, can you?" said Freddie.

"Let's leave our bikes here," said Nan.

Bert was first down the sandy path. When he got to the shack, he saw that it was raised up on stilts. A creaky ladder leaned against the doorway.

The others came up behind him.

"Think we can get in?" said Freddie.

"I'll try," said Bert, climbing up.

He leaned against the door. It fell in.

The others scrambled up the ladder and went into the shack. It was filled with rusty pieces of metal. They were bent in all sorts of strange shapes.

"The gold has to be here," said Bert.

They searched the shack. They turned over every piece of rusty metal. But no gold.

"This is where 'X marks the spot,'" said Bert, looking at the map. "Hey, maybe it's buried!"

They climbed down the ladder and crawled under the shack.

"No room to use the shovel." Bert frowned.

"We can use the trowel," said Freddie.

"We'll take turns," said Nan.

"I'll go first," said Flossie.

"It's my trowel," said Freddie. He started to dig.

But soon Freddie became tired. He gave the trowel to Bert.

"I'll dig for a while over here," said Bert. Bert dug until the hole was a few feet deep. Then he handed the trowel to Nan.

"I'll try here," Nan said. She started to dig in a new spot. But she had no luck.

Flossie's turn was no better.

"Okay," Freddie said. "I'm ready to start again." He took the trowel and began a new hole.

"I don't think this is going to work," said Flossie.

"Wait a minute!" shouted Freddie. "I've hit something."

He dug around with his hands. At last he brought up a glass jar.

"There's a note inside," said Bert.

Freddie opened the jar and took out the note. He read it aloud.

" 'Stop looking for things that don't belong to you.' "

"Looks like someone's trying to tell us something," said Bert.

"You know," Freddie said. "This is a Micro-Man peanut butter jar."

"Micro-Man peanut butter? I didn't know they made such a thing," said Nan.

"They don't. I mean it's the brand of peanut butter that has the labels you save. To get a Micro-Man Decoder Program free."

"Do you hear anything?" interjected Bert. "Are those waves getting louder?"

They crawled out from under the shack and looked around. The tide had come in while they were searching. Water was lapping at the edges of the sand around the shack. The strip of sand they'd crossed earlier was under water.

"I guess that's why they call it Dunking Neck," said Nan.

"Now we know why they built the shack on stilts," said Freddie.

"Brrrr, it's getting cold," Flossie said. "Listen to that wind howl."

"We'll be stranded out here unless someone comes and gets us," said Nan.

"How can they?" Bert said. "No one knows where we are!"

8

Sink or Swim

"We're going to freeze to death!" moaned Flossie.

"But first we'll drown," said Freddie.

"We could try to build a fire," Nan said. "Then we could use it to signal for help."

"We don't have any matches," said Freddie.

"Never mind all that," Bert said. "We have to make a run for it. We can swim the rest of the way. But we've got to do it now before the tide gets higher. You kids can touch bottom when you get tired."

"Come on," Nan said, grabbing Flossie by the hand. "Let's go!"

They ran down to the end of the beach.

Nan was the first to wade into the water. It reached the cuffs of her jeans. Then her shins. Then her knees. By that time it was up to Flossie's waist.

A fog had rolled in. Foghorns moaned in the distance.

"Can . . . can you see land yet?" asked Flossie.

"Keep going!" shouted Bert from the rear.

"Grab my waist," Nan said to Flossie. "Float behind me until I start swimming."

"You hold on to me," Bert said to Freddie.

They slogged forward until the water was too high.

"Hey," Bert shouted, "I can see our bikes."

"We can make it," cried Nan. "We just have to swim a little way. Kick those legs, Flossie. We're almost there."

A few moments later they were out of the water. It felt great to be on dry land again. Even if they were soaking wet.

And there, standing next to their bikes, was Mr. Reade. A pair of binoculars was slung around his neck.

"Would you please tell me what you were doing on my property?" he asked.

"Your property?" said Nan.

"Yes," he said. "Dunking Neck is part of the Wilson estate. You were trespassing. Now, I'd like to know what you were doing there."

Before the Bobbseys could answer, Pete Smedley's old truck pulled up. He opened the door and got out.

"Been looking for you kids everywhere," he said. "Your mother came home and found nobody there. So I had to come out after you."

"How'd you know we were here?" asked Freddie.

"Everyone in town saw you riding out this way. Nowhere else you could've been going," said Pete.

Mr. Reade was about to start scolding them again. But Pete said, "You're going to catch your death of cold. Get in back. Right now."

They scrambled into the back of the truck, bikes and all. Mr. Reade glared at them as the truck drove off.

"Kind of bumpy," said Flossie, sitting on a bag of grass seed.

"Beats pedaling with wet pants," said Bert.

Freddie sneezed.

Mr. Reade turns up at the oddest times, Nan thought as the truck rolled along. I suppose he heard we were out here, too. But he didn't have to spy on us with those binoculars.

The binoculars! The flash of light! The man up on the cliff above the house . . . maybe that was Mr. Reade, too!

She hunkered down in the corner, among Pete's rusty shovels and bits of pipe.

The truck came to a sudden stop. They were home.

"Where on earth have you been?" asked Mrs. Bobbsey. "You look like you're almost drowned. Quick, get out of those clothes and dry off."

"I'm going to take a hot shower," said Freddie.

"And I'm really going to soak in the tub this time," said Flossie.

Bert and Nan quickly changed their clothes. They were soon seated at the kitchen table drinking hot cocoa.

"What happened?" asked Mrs. Bobbsey.

Nan told her about Bert's finding the map in the barn.

"And then Freddie found a jar," said Bert. He told her about the note.

"Someone is trying to make you kids look silly," she said.

"But, Mom," protested Nan. "There's a mystery here."

"Don't 'But, Mom' me," Mrs. Bobbsey said. "This mystery could be dangerous. You took a foolish chance today. And you made Mr. Reade angry."

"But we *have* to investigate," said Freddie from the doorway. He walked into the kitchen, followed by Flossie.

"I know better than to expect you to stop." Mrs. Bobbsey shook her head, trying to hide a smile. "But couldn't you try to do it more carefully?"

"I'm always careful around ghosts," Flossie said.

Mr. Bobbsey banged the screen door.

"Ghosts?" He laughed. *"And* buried treasure. I'm glad you're having fun."

Bert told him what had happened at the shack.

"Jim Reade has a lot on his mind," Mr. Bobbsey said. "Why don't you spend some time with Jimmy?"

"How can we?" Bert said. "He's never around. I've never even seen him."

"Neither have I," said Flossie.

"You're not missing anything," said Freddie.

"Do you think he's afraid of competition?" Nan asked. "I mean, the sand-castle contest?"

"He might just be shy," Mrs. Bobbsey said.

"Now, there's something else we have to talk about. What do you say to pizza for dinner? In front of the TV?"

"There's nothing on but reruns," said Flossie.

"That's why I rented a videotape," Mr. Bobbsey said. "Anybody up for *Intergalactic Intrigue?*"

"Great!" said Bert and Nan.

"My favorite!" shouted Freddie.

"Yippee!" said Flossie.

Later on, they were all settled in front of the TV.

The music began. Spaceships soared through the skies. Two collided in a burst of flame.

Then suddenly: darkness.

It was not just the TV that was dark, but the whole room.

All of the lights had gone out. The house was plunged into blackness.

9

Ghosts Again?

"Do we have any candles?"

"I'll get a flashlight."

"I forgot to pack mine."

"Everybody stay put!"

Voices tumbled over one another as the Bobbseys fumbled in the darkness.

But Bert rushed into action. He charged out the front door to the cellar door.

There, by the light of the moon, he saw someone.

He made his move, a flying tackle . . . and down came the target. It was a redheaded boy, pale and shaking.

"Don't hit me!" the boy said. "I didn't do anything. Honest!"

"Who are you?" demanded Bert.

"I . . . I'm Jimmy Reade."

"What are you doing out here?"

"I . . . I just wanted to scare you a little. I . . . I was going to pretend to be a g-g-ghost. My dad told me that you heard about the Wilsons. So, I just thought . . ."

"You thought you'd scare us by putting us in the dark, didn't you?" said Bert.

"No! I swear I didn't touch the lights. The real g-g-ghost did that!"

"The *real* ghost? You expect me to believe that?"

"It's the truth, honest. I saw it all in white, coming out of the cellar. Just before you got here. I was running from the ghost, not from you. The ghost must have put out the lights." He froze.

"What's the matter?" said Bert. Then he saw his father coming up from the cellar.

"Thought it was another ghost, huh?" Bert said to Jimmy.

"I came down the inside stairs," said Mr. Bobbsey, pointing his flashlight at the two boys. "What do we have here?"

He listened as Jimmy repeated the story he had told Bert.

"That was no ghost. Someone turned off the circuit breaker. Then he cut the cables," Mr. Bobbsey said. "I won't be able to fix it till tomorrow.

"But your mother found some candles, Bert. You'd better go back inside. Meanwhile, I'll drive Jimmy home. I'll report this to the police on the way back."

Inside, Bert found everyone huddled around the kitchen table, where Mrs. Bobbsey had placed a lit candle.

"It's late," said Mrs. Bobbsey. "The only thing to do is go to bed."

"Good night, Mom," said Flossie.

"Wherever you are," said Freddie.

Mrs. Bobbsey laughed. "Good night, kids."

"Let's just pop in your room for a minute," Bert said to Flossie when they got upstairs.

The children arranged themselves on the bed. Enough moonlight came in through the windows so they could see each other.

"All right," Nan said. "Let's see if we can figure out what's going on."

"There are a lot of pieces that don't fit together," Bert said. "Let's make a list of the clues."

"There's my broken mirror," Flossie said. "The ghost doesn't care about seven years of bad luck."

"Then there's the piece of pipe. The one holding down the root cellar doors," said Bert.

"What about that rubber ring-thing I found?" asked Flossie.

"The washer?" Nan said. "I don't know if we could call that a clue."

"There was that seaweed on your window-sill," said Flossie.

"And what about that map? And the note inside the Micro-Man peanut butter jar?"

"It might have fingerprints," said Bert.

"Jimmy's, I bet," Freddie said. "Mr. Reade told us he was a Micro-Man fan."

"Could be," Nan said. "But we left the jar behind. I have the map and the note, but they got soaked. You can't even tell what they are anymore."

"Hmmm," Bert said. "I can't see what all those things add up to."

"Neither can I," said Nan.

"What about suspects?" asked Flossie.

"I bet that little rat Jimmy played the map trick on us and put out the lights," Freddie said.

"He said he didn't touch the lights and I believe him. He was really frightened by the ghost," said Bert.

"What about Mr. Reade?" said Nan. "He was watching the house with his binoculars. And he keeps turning up at odd times."

"So does Pete," Flossie said. "But I'm glad he gave us a ride. Even if his truck is a junkyard."

"I don't know," Nan said. "The pieces and the people don't connect. Something's missing."

"Sure," Freddie said. "The gold."

"That does it," Nan said. "Let's sleep on it."

The next morning they decided to put all the loose ends aside. This was the day of the sand-castle contest.

"Let's head for the beach and start piling up the sand," said Freddie.

"I'm going to take a ride with Dad first," Flossie said. "He's going over to Pete's house to borrow something."

"See you later," said Nan. She went to join her brothers.

All over the beach strange shapes rose from the sand. The children of Beachcliff Bay were hard at work.

By the time Flossie got back, the Bobbsey

sand-castle entry was almost finished. Freddie was helping Nan and Bert put on the finishing touches by not getting in their way. He saw Flossie first. She was carrying something. A thick book with a pea-soup green cover!

"Hey, that's the library book!" Freddie said. "Where'd you get it?"

"I borrowed it," said Flossie.

"From the library?" asked Nan.

Flossie shook her head. "I found it in Pete's garage. Daddy made me wait outside while he went in to see Pete. So I walked around. And I saw the book in the garage. And there was a picture of our house inside."

"So you just took it," Bert said. "What if he notices it's missing?"

"Well," Flossie said, "it's not his book, is it?"

"It's the same one we found in the library," said Nan, flipping the pages.

"You did a great drawing," said Freddie.

"It looks just like the house in the book," Bert said. "There's that funny porch. And the trellis. And the whale on top."

"That's not a whale," Freddie said. "That's a fish. Ours is a whale."

"Are you sure?" asked Bert. He whipped out his Rex Sleuther magnifying glass. "You're right, Freddie. The weather vane in the book is different."

74

"That means the one on the house is new, sort of," said Nan.

"Then why doesn't it move?" asked Flossie.

"Because maybe it's not a weather vane. It might be something else," Bert said.

"Clay Wilson was a sculptor," said Nan.

"And Jennie was a painter," said Freddie.

"Do you suppose," Bert said, "that it's made of gold?"

10

Go for the Gold

Bert heard someone groan behind him.

He turned and looked, but he was too late.

Whoever had heard what they said had run off.

"I can see legs," Freddie said. "They're going toward our house!"

"Come on!" cried Bert. "We can't let him get away."

"Don't worry," shouted Nan. "I know who it is."

"You do?" said Bert, stopping in his tracks.

"Yes," Nan said. "But let's make sure we're right about the gold, first."

"Follow me," Freddie said. "We'll take my secret tunnel through the grass and beat whoever that is back to the house."

The other Bobbseys ran after Freddie into the tunnel formed by the long grass.

Within moments they came out near the back of the house.

"Quiet!" Nan said. "Do you hear that?"

"Sounds like something banging against the house," said Bert.

"I bet it's a ladder," said Freddie.

"Look!" Flossie said. "Someone is climbing up the side of the house."

"It's . . . it's Pete!" Bert said. "He's got a crowbar."

"He's going to knock down the weather vane."

By now, Pete had reached the roof. He yanked at the weather vane, but it wouldn't come off.

He grabbed the crowbar and swung it at the rusty base. The whale shook loose and fell. Pete grabbed for it, but missed.

The whale toppled off the roof. It hit the driveway and cracked open.

"Look at that shiny part," shouted Flossie. "It's the gold!"

While the others stared at the broken whale, Bert dashed over to the ladder. He yanked it away from the house.

"Hey!" Pete shouted. "Put that back! I was trying to fix the weather vane."

"I'll just bet you were," called Nan. Then, she whispered to Flossie, "Go inside and call the police."

"You heard us down on the beach, didn't you?" Nan said. "You realized your book was missing—the one you stole from the library. And you figured out Flossie took it. So you came looking for it."

"Why'd he steal it in the first place?" asked Bert.

"To keep us from finding out too much about Wilson House and looking for the gold," Nan said. "He's been after that gold himself."

"He's the ghost?" asked Freddie.

"I'm sure of it," said Nan.

"The pipe could have been part of his plumbing stuff," said Bert.

"And that ring-thing I found . . ." said Flossie, who had just returned from the house.

"Right! The washer. That's plumbing, too," said Freddie.

"Who knew his way around Wilson House

better than Pete?" Nan said. "He could easily sneak in and out. I'll bet he made all those weird noises in the secret passage."

"Sure," Bert said. "He knew about electricity, too. And exactly where to cut off the power."

"What about the map? And the Micro-Man peanut butter jar? Think he did that, too?" asked Freddie.

"We'll find out soon enough. Here are the police," said Nan. A Beachcliff Bay police car stopped in the driveway.

"I'm Deputy Chief Morris," said the driver after he got out. "What's going on here?"

"Those crazy kids won't let me down!" shouted Pete.

Nan explained what had happened. She pointed to the broken weather vane lying in the driveway. The golden pieces glistened in the sun.

"I've heard enough to be convinced that something's fishy," Deputy Chief Morris said. "Let's get Pete down. I have some questions I want to ask him."

Nan and Bert propped the ladder against the house. Pete climbed down carefully.

"You little varmints!" he shouted at the Bobbseys.

"Wait a second, Pete Smedley," Deputy Chief

Morris said. "Why have you been racing all over town lately? You broke the speed limit on the road to Dunking Neck early yesterday morning. And then you did it again later on in the day!"

"I had things to do," muttered Pete.

"Sure," Nan said. "First you hid the map in the shed and planted that warning note in the jar under the shack. Then you came back to the shack to see if we'd found it!"

"I did not! I came back to make sure you didn't drown out there!" shouted Pete.

"Wait a minute," Nan said. "Are you saying you didn't try to scare us away from Wilson House because of the gold?"

"And why shouldn't I?" cried Pete. "It was my gold, too! Clay and Jennie would never have got away with the robbery without me waiting for them in the car."

"So you drove the getaway car!" said Bert.

"But did they give me my share? No. They tell me it's not safe. They'll take care of it, hide it somewhere. But they don't tell me where.

"Then the cops get wind of it, and Clay and Jennie try to get away. But I seen them leave. They didn't take nothing with them. Didn't have time. The gold's around here somewhere, I says to myself after they drowned."

"So you started looking for it," Nan said. "But people came to stay. You made up the ghost stories to scare them off. And it worked."

"You used the secret passage, didn't you?" asked Bert.

"Sure," Pete said. "Nobody knew about it, and nobody figured the gold might be around here. Till you kids started snooping around."

Flossie giggled.

"Don't laugh, you little pest," snapped Pete. "Figured I'd get you all out of the house right away when I smashed that mirror."

"And sneaked down the secret passage afterward," said Flossie.

"Where did you get that Micro-Man peanut butter jar?" asked Freddie.

"The Reade kid left it when his father was working on the house."

"Enough," said Deputy Chief Morris. "You're under arrest.

"Kids, don't touch that whale. We'll need it for evidence. I'll send someone over for it." Deputy Chief Morris read Pete his rights. Then they drove off.

Bert turned to Nan.

"You know, I thought it might be Mr. Reade," he said. "Why would he be watching us with his binoculars?"

"I know!" Flossie said. "Daddy told me when I went for the ride with him. Mr. Reade uses them to look at birds."

"A birdwatcher," Nan said. "That explains what he was doing up on that hill. As well as out at Dunking Neck."

"I wish it could have been Jimmy. I still say he's a little rat," Freddie said.

"He'll probably turn out not to be so bad after all," said Nan.

"Here are Mom and Dad," Bert said. "Wait till they see this pile of gold."

"You're all okay?" asked Mr. Bobbsey, rushing over. "Deputy Chief Morris called me at Mr. Reade's office from his car and told me what had happened."

"Your father picked me up at the library," Mrs. Bobbsey said. "Did you know Mrs. Morris is one of the judges in the sand-castle contest?"

"The contest!" Nan said. "We might not be too late. Mom . . . Dad . . . will you keep an eye on the gold till the police come back? But don't touch it—it's evidence."

"Off you go. I'll stand guard," said Mr. Bobbsey.

"I'm going inside," Mrs. Bobbsey said. "I found my story. To think, it was right under . . . No, make that *on top of* our own roof."

The Bobbsey sand castle was still standing down on the beach. But there was no time to add the finishing touches. Or to fix it. One side had caved in.

"I'm sorry, the judging is over," said Mrs. Morris, walking over to them. "But the work you did was very impressive. So we've awarded you an Honorable Mention."

"That's great," Nan said. "Considering it wasn't finished."

"And that side caved in," said Bert.

"I'm sorry about that. Jimmy Reade tried to kick down your entry. He damaged that side. Of course, his entry was disqualified. His father was quite angry with him."

"I told you," Freddie said. "He's a little—"

"We know!" said the other three Bobbseys.

"Besides," added Flossie. "What do we care? While he was cheating to get the gold medal, we found the real gold!"

"And it was a whale of a find," said Freddie.

Everybody laughed.